KU-365-971

This book belongs to:

....

....

....

....

Retold by Gaby Goldsack
Illustrated by Kim Blundell

Language consultant: Betty Root

This edition published by Parragon in 2013
Parragon
Chartist House
15–17 Trim Street
Bath BA1 1HA, UK
www.parragon.com

Copyright © Parragon Books Ltd 2002

All rights reserved. No part of this publication may be reproduced, stored in a retrieval system or transmitted, in any form or by any means, electronic, mechanical, photocopying, recording or otherwise, without the prior permission of the copyright holder.

ISBN 978-1-4454-7067-2

Printed in China

The Three Billy Goats Gruff

Bath · New York · Singapore · Hong Kong · Cologne · Delhi
Melbourne · Amsterdam · Johannesburg · Shenzhen

Helping Your Child to Read

Learning to read is an exciting challenge for most children. From a very early age, sharing story books with children, talking about the pictures and guessing what might happen next are all very important parts of the reading experience.

Sharing reading

Set aside a regular quiet time to share reading with younger children, or to be on hand to encourage older children as they develop into independent readers.

This book is intended to encourage and support the early stages of learning to read. It is a well-loved tale that children will happily listen to again and again. Familiarity helps children to identify some of the words and phrases.

When you feel your child is ready to move on a little, encourage them to join in so that you read the story aloud together. Always pause to talk about the pictures. The easy-to-read speech bubbles in this book provide an excellent 'joining-in' activity. The bright, clear illustrations and matching text will help children to understand the story.

Building confidence

In time, children will want to read *to* you. When this happens, be patient and give continual praise. They may not read all the words correctly, but children's substitutions are often very good guesses.

The repetition in each book is particularly helpful for building confidence. If your child cannot read a particular word, go back to the beginning of the sentence and read it together so the meaning is not lost. Most importantly, do not continue if your child is tired or simply in need of a change.

Reading alone

The next step is to ask your child to read alone. Try to be on hand to give help and support. Remember to give lots of encouragement and praise. This will ensure that children will find reading an enjoyable and rewarding experience.

8

Once upon a time there were three Billy Goats Gruff.

There was a big Billy Goat Gruff.

There was a middle-sized Billy Goat Gruff.

And there was a little Billy Goat Gruff.

I am a little goat.

The three goats all loved to eat grass.

They ate grass all day long on the hill.
But they never crossed the bridge to eat
the grass on the other side.

They never crossed the bridge because the Troll lived under the bridge.

The Troll was very bad. He ate anyone who dared to cross his bridge.

One day, the little Billy Goat Gruff looked at the green, green grass on the other side of the bridge.

"I'm not scared of a silly old Troll," he said. "I'm going to cross the bridge."

"Me too," said the middle-sized Billy Goat Gruff.

"And me," said the big Billy Goat Gruff.

"You go first. It was your idea," said the big Billy Goat Gruff to the little Billy Goat Gruff.

Trip, trap, trip, trip, trip, trap!

So the little Billy Goat Gruff set off across the bridge.

Trip, trap, trip, trip, trap went his hooves.

"Who is that trip-trapping over my bridge?" roared the Troll.

"It's only me!" said the little Billy Goat Gruff. "I'm going to eat the green, green grass on the other side of the bridge."

"Oh no, you're not!" roared the Troll. "I'm going to eat you up!"

"But I am just little," said the little Billy Goat Gruff. "Wait until my middle-sized brother comes across. He is far bigger than me."

"Very well!" said the Troll.

Very well!

So the little Billy Goat Gruff crossed the bridge. Soon he was eating the green, green grass.

Next, the middle-sized Billy Goat Gruff crossed the bridge.

"Who is that trip-trapping over my bridge?" roared the Troll.

"It's only me!" said the middle-sized Billy Goat Gruff. "I am going to eat the green, green grass on the other side of the bridge."

"Oh no, you're not!" roared the Troll. "I'm going to eat you up!"

I'm going to eat you up!

"But I am just middle-sized," said the middle-sized Billy Goat Gruff. "Wait until my big brother comes across. He is far bigger than me."

"Very well!" said the Troll.

And don't come back!

So the middle-sized Billy Goat Gruff
crossed the bridge. Soon he was eating
the green, green grass.

Next, the big Billy Goat Gruff crossed the bridge.

Quake! Shake! Rumble!

"Who is that trip-trapping over my bridge?" roared the Troll.

"It's only me!" said the big Billy Goat Gruff. "I'm going to eat the green, green grass on the other side of the bridge."

"Oh no, you're not!" roared the Troll. "I'm going to eat you up!"

The Troll jumped onto the bridge.

The big Billy Goat Gruff lowered his horns and charged.

Crash! The big Billy Goat Gruff banged into the Troll. The Troll flew into the air. Splash! He fell into the water.

Take that!

Crash!
Splash!

The big Billy Goat Gruff skipped over the bridge. Soon he was eating the green, green grass.

And the ugly Troll was never seen again.

Hooray!

Read and Say

How many of these words can you say?
The pictures will help you. Look back in
your book and see if you can find the
words in the story.

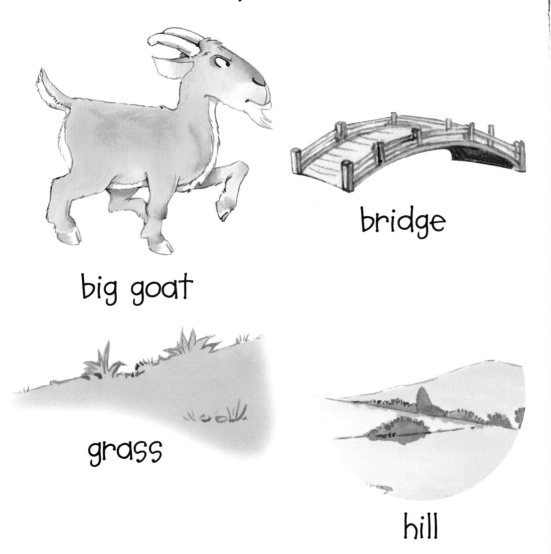

big goat

bridge

grass

hill

hooves

horns

little goat

middle-sized goat

Troll

water

29

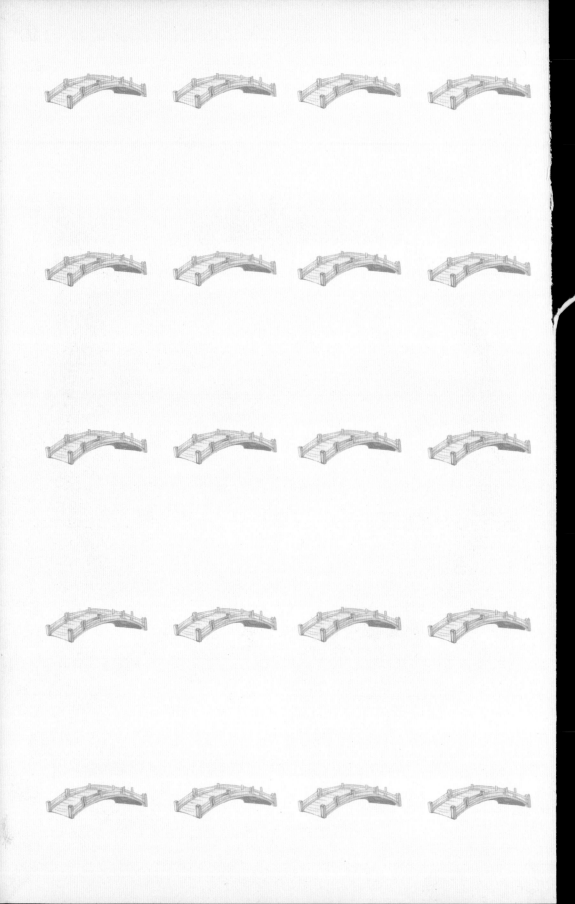